For Milo and Alfie – M.R.

For Julia x – T.B.

Published in the UK by Scholastic, 2025
Scholastic, Bosworth Avenue, Warwick, CV34 6UQ
Scholastic Ireland, 89E Lagan Road, Dublin Industrial Estate, Glasnevin, Dublin, D11 HP5F

SCHOLASTIC and associated logos are trademarks and/or
registered trademarks of Scholastic Inc.

Text © Michelle Robinson, 2025
Cover and inside illustrations © Tim Budgen, 2025

The moral rights of Michelle Robinson and Tim Budgen have been asserted by them.

ISBN 978 0702 33905 9

A CIP catalogue record for this book is available from the British Library.

All rights reserved.
This book is sold subject to the condition that it shall not, by way of trade or otherwise, be lent, hired out or otherwise circulated in any form of binding or cover other than that in which it is published. No part of this publication may be reproduced, stored in a retrieval system, or transmitted in any form or by any other means (electronic, mechanical, photocopying, recording or otherwise) or used to train any artificial intelligence technologies without prior written permission of Scholastic Limited. Subject to EU law Scholastic Limited expressly reserves this work from the text and data mining exception.

Printed in China
Paper made from wood grown in sustainable forests and other controlled sources.

1 3 5 7 9 10 8 6 4 2

This is a work of fiction. Any resemblance to actual people, events or locales is entirely coincidental.

www.scholastic.co.uk

For safety or quality concerns:
UK: www.scholastic.co.uk/productinformation
EU: www.scholastic.ie/productinformation

THE SNAPPY SHARK

MICHELLE ROBINSON
& TIM BUDGEN

Scholastic

"Sure! Come join the fun!
We're all playing **hide-and-seek!"**
Enjoy it, everyone.

Toot the turtle starts to count.

All the others hide.

Mark picks out a coral reef and tries to squeeze inside.

"**Found you!**" Toot says quickly.
Mark's **NOT** a happy chap.

Mind your temper, Mark the shark.

Mark... is... going... to...

...SNAP!

"I WASN'T READY!"
Mark complains.

Toot begins to cry.

Sid the squid says quickly, "Let's give something **else** a try..."

Be a good sport, Mark the shark. *Please* don't spoil the fun.
Time for **painting pictures** next. Enjoy it, everyone.

Mark is doing pretty well. His picture makes him proud!

Until a little spillage makes him holler **really loud.**

"IT'S NOT FAIR! YOU RUINED IT!"
Mark's **NOT** a happy chap.
Steady on now, Mark the shark.

Mark... is... going... to...

Mark the shark swims off at once, keen to get stuck in.
"Let's make this a contest," Mark says, hoping he will win.

"Who can find the **best** shell?

And the **BIGGEST**?

And the **MOST**?"

Mark finds an **enormous** one. He's just about to boast . . .

When Raff the ray says happily,
"I found a pearl in mine!"

Please be gracious, Mark the shark.
It's not your time to shine.

"IT ISN'T FAIR! YOU CHEATED!" Mark says, getting in a flap.
Take it easy, Mark the shark.

Mark... is... going... to...

...SNAP!

He bares his teeth at Raff the ray. But Raff is standing **TOUGH.**

"No more snapping," he tells Mark.
"Play nice, we've had **enough.**

Being snapped at *isn't* fun.
It's **NOT** what good friends do.
Be a little kinder, or we won't play games with you."

"FINE!" Mark snaps. He swims away.
"I DIDN'T *WANT* TO PLAY!"

He slinks into a cave and sulks.

"Who needs friends anyway?"

Mark has **lots of feelings** and they're often really **strong.**
It sometimes makes it hard for him to know when he is wrong.

Now he's all alone, Mark has some quiet time to think.

"I made my friends feel bad," he says.

His heart begins to **sink.**

"I must control my temper."

Nice slow **breaths.**

Count **one, two,**

three . . .

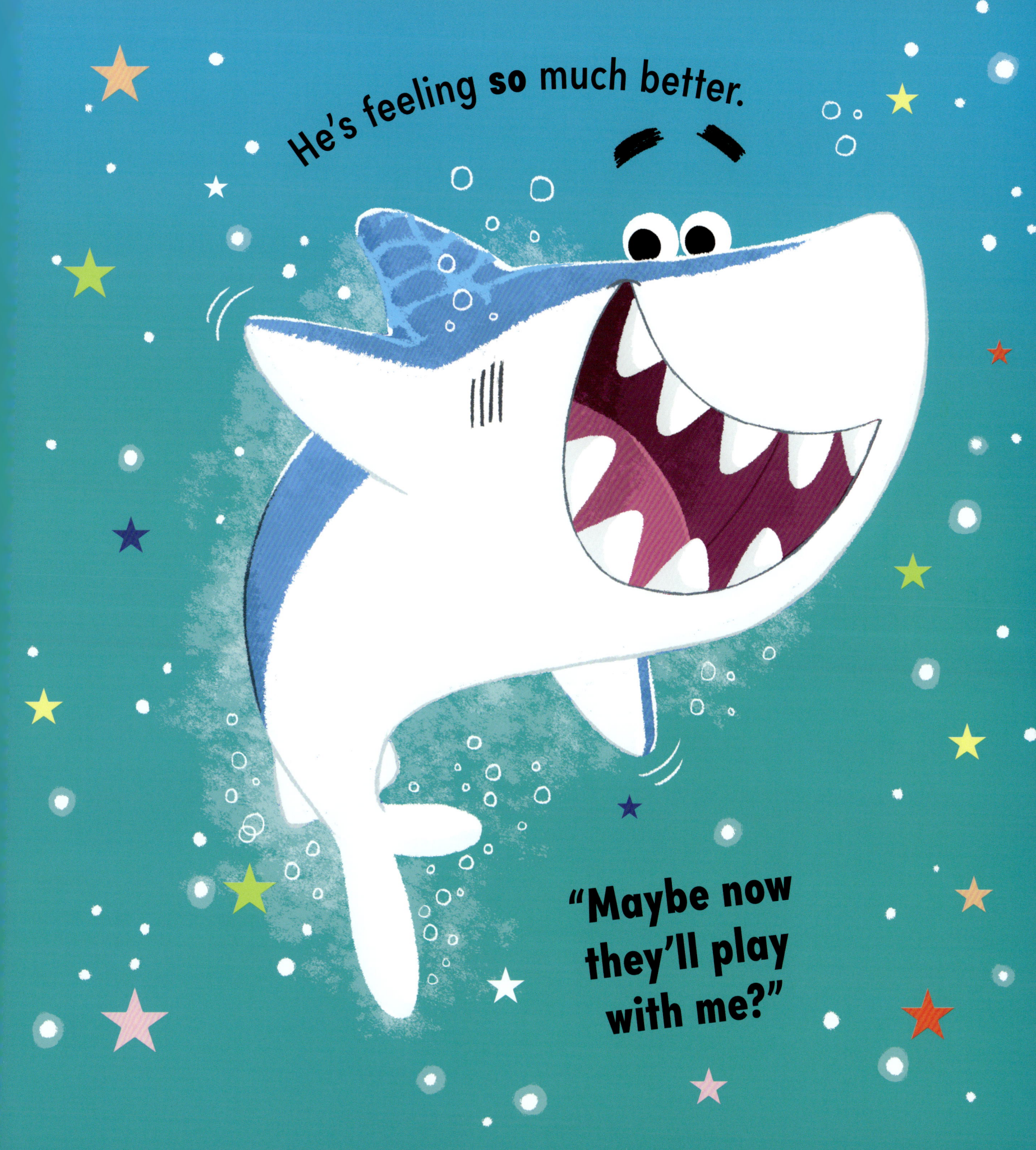

"I hope you can forgive me?" says the calmer, kinder shark. The coral kids are **thrilled** to see this newly mindful Mark.

"I'll **NEVER** snap again," he says, "I really, truly mean it."

They're busy having fun.

Do you think anybody's seen it . . . ?

Will he...? Might he...?

"I really had to snap that time. Is everyone okay?"

Toot and Sid and Raff all cheer. **"You're really AWESOME, Mark!** *Everyone* snaps sometimes. **You're one very special shark."**

Mark the shark's a **brand-new fish.** He's learned to take it *easy.*

Any stress? He takes a **breath** and soon, he's **bright** and **breezy.**

SNAP! LOOK OUT!
It's Mark the shark.

He **loves** to play games with his friends!

Until, when things don't go to plan, Mark starts to feel a bit **wobbly** and he . . .

SNAAAAPS!

But when there's a commotion in the ocean, can Mark channel his big emotions and use his **SNAP** to save the day?

The perfect story to reassure children that we **all** have wobbles sometimes, and that's OK.

ISBN 978-0-702339-05-9

£7.99

SCHOLASTIC
scholastic.co.uk